TEDD ARNOLD

HUGGLY'S®
THANKSGIVING PARADE

SCHOLASTIC INC. Cartwheel BOOKS®

New York   Toronto   London   Auckland   Sydney
Mexico City   New Delhi   Hong Kong   Buenos Aires

For Grace, who first invited Huggly into the people world.
Thank you!
— T.A.

Copyright © 2002 by Tedd Arnold.
All rights reserved. Published by Scholastic Inc.
HUGGLY and THE MONSTER UNDER THE BED are trademarks and/or registered trademarks of Tedd Arnold.
SCHOLASTIC, CARTWHEEL BOOKS, and associated
logos are trademarks and/or registered trademarks of Scholastic Inc.

0-439-32450-5

Library of Congress Cataloging-in-Publication Data Available

12 11 10 9 8 7 6 5 4 3 2 1   02 03 04 05 06

Printed in the U.S.A.   24
First printing, November 2002

Huggly loved playing tag with his friends Booter and Grubble.

"Tag! You're it, Grubble!" yelled Huggly.

"Hey, guys," said Booter. "Don't you think we've gone too far from our Secret Slime Pit?"

Huggly and Grubble looked around.
"Yeah," said Grubble. "I don't recognize this place."
"Hey!" said Huggly. "Look down there!"
The three friends gazed down a side tunnel.

They followed it and entered an open cavern with many hatchways in the ceiling. They knew that hatchways always opened underneath beds in the people world.

"We gotta check this out!" Huggly whispered.

"Yeah, no kidding," said Grubble.

"Okay," said Booter, "but then we go back home!"

Huggly led his friends up steps in the middle of the cavern. They climbed out from under a bed in a huge room filled with beds.

"Where are we now?" asked Huggly.

Booter saw a sign. "I've heard about places like this," she said. "People get their beds and other stuff here."

"Tag! You're it, Huggly!" yelled Grubble.
Huggly chased after both of his friends. They leapt from bed to bed, bouncing and laughing themselves silly.

Suddenly they heard noise, music, and voices.
Huggly hurried to a window.

"What's going on out there?" he said. Booter and
Grubble hurried over to look.

They could see tall buildings. Outside the buildings,
crowds of people hurried every which way. Many were dressed
to look silly. Others were starting to play music.

"It looks like they're getting ready for a big party,"
said Huggly.

"Yeah!" said Grubble. "Let's join them."

"But we aren't supposed to be seen by people," said
Booter. "We might get caught."

"Some of those people are dressed to look like
creatures," said Huggly. "So maybe they won't notice us."

The three friends hurried downstairs to a door that led outside.

Huggly, Booter, and Grubble walked among the busy people. No one paid them any attention. They found a pile of dress-up clothes. Many people were grabbing things to wear.

DELIVERY ENTRANCE

By the time they reached the pile, there were only hats left for the three monsters.

"Hey, you!" said a booming people voice behind them.

"*Oh, no!*" thought Huggly. "*We've been caught!*"

They turned around, holding their breath in fear.
A big people guy was standing there.

"You looking for something to wear?" he said,
handing each of them a shoulder bag. "Wear these.
And during the Thanksgiving Parade, walk beside one
of those floats and throw candy to all the children you
see." He walked away.

The three monsters let out a deep breath.

"Whew!" said Booter. "That was close!"

"What's a parade?" asked Grubble.

"I don't know," said Huggly. He pointed at a line of decorated vehicles. "Maybe those things make a parade."

People were climbing onto the Thanksgiving Parade floats. More people, dressed alike, were lining up and testing their musical instruments. Booter, Grubble, and Huggly walked around, looking at all the wonderful sights.

Huggly dropped farther and farther behind his friends. He gazed at a particularly beautiful float.

Suddenly Huggly realized that he was standing alone in the middle of some kind of colorful, wrinkly stuff.

He heard a hissing sound and the stuff started to
billow up around him. Huggly tried to run, but he tripped
over a rope and fell on his face.

Before Huggly could get up, he felt himself being lifted
off the ground.

"Booter! Grubble! Help!" cried Huggly.
But Booter and Grubble couldn't hear him.
Huggly went higher and higher.

He realized he was on top of something that was rising toward the sky. Booter and Grubble waved, but Huggly was too scared to let go and wave back.

Below, the musicians were marching. They started playing music. The floats began rolling. The parade started moving down the street. People were cheering.

The thing Huggly was sitting on stopped rising and started moving! People on the ground were pulling it with ropes. Below, Booter and Grubble wondered what to do.

Huggly held on tight and sailed between tall buildings. He was beginning to enjoy himself. Never had he seen so many happy people. He saw more of the big things pulled by ropes. Each one was different.

Suddenly Huggly heard voices nearby. There were people
in the windows of all the tall buildings, watching the
parade. When they saw Huggly, they waved at him and
cheered.

Huggly was delighted. Without thinking, he let go and
waved back. Just then a gust of wind blew. It shook the big
floating thing.

Huggly tried to grab hold again, but it was too late. He started sliding faster and faster. Then he was tumbling through the air. People in the windows and people watching from below all cried, "O-o-o-oh!"

Below, Booter and Grubble had been tossing candy to children. But they were keeping an eye on Huggly. When he fell, they rushed this way and that way trying to get in position to catch him.

Finally they climbed onto a float to get under Huggly—just in time! He landed in their arms—*WHUMP*! The float caved in beneath them. The crowds of people cried, "O-o-o-oh!"

The parade stopped! The music stopped! The cheering stopped! Everyone held their breath.

Finally, Huggly, Booter, and Grubble struggled out of the hole in the float. They were okay! The crowds of people sighed, "Ah-h-h-h!"

Then everyone cheered, louder than ever. They shouted, "Good show! Bravo!" Everyone waved. The monsters waved back. Music started and the floats rolled down the street once again.

"Thanksgiving Parades are fun!" said Huggly.

"I agree," said Grubble

"Me, too," said Booter.

When the parade was over, the three friends dropped what they were wearing and escaped into the building with all the beds. They dived under the bed in the middle of the room.

Once they were back in the monster world, they sat down to catch their breath.

"I have something for you both," Huggly said to his friends. He opened his hands and candy spilled out. "I know we're not supposed to take people stuff, but they were giving it away to everybody."

"Thank you," said Grubble. "I didn't get to eat anything during the parade."

"Yeah!" said Booter. "Thanks."

"No. I want to thank *you*," said Huggly, "for saving me! You will always be my best friends. Thank you! Thank you! Thank you!"